Illustrated by Derry Dillon

First published
April 05 in Great Britain by

PUBLISHING

© **Sandra Glover 2005**

The moral right of the author has been asserted in accordance with the
Copyright, Designs and Patents Act 1988

ISBN-10: 1 904904 30 0
ISBN-13: 978 1 904904 30 4

Educational Printing Services Limited
Albion Mill, Water Street, Great Harwood, Blackburn BB6 7QR
Telephone: (01254) 882080   Fax: (01254) 882010
E-mail: enquiries@eprint.co.uk   Website: www.eprint.co.uk

Contents

Chapter 1
The School Newspaper

I blame Miss Harris for what happened. I mean, it was her idea to do the school newspaper, wasn't it?

'Won't that be fun, Year 6?' she said, beaming at us.

'Strange idea of fun, she's got,' I whispered to Joss.

1

But to my surprise, Joss was looking quite interested.

'*And,*' Miss Harris added, glaring at us. 'We can raise money for school by selling our paper at the Summer Gala.'

'But that's less than two weeks away!' I said.

'Yes, Scott, it is,' she said. 'Real newspapers work to deadlines and so must we. Now we're going to work in pairs. Some of us will be in the advertising department, some of us will be reporters . . . '

'Fashion!' screeched Emma. 'Me and Kelly want to be fashion reporters.'

'Cookery column.'

'Adverts.'

'Films.'

People were calling out ideas faster
than Miss Harris could write their names on
the board.

'What about you, Scott?' Miss Harris asked, when the board was almost full.

'Dunno,' I said.

Greg and Nibsy had grabbed sport and there was nothing else I fancied.

'I've got an idea!' screeched Joss. 'Crime! Scott and me will be crime reporters.'

Trust my mate, Joss, to come up with a daft idea like that. We live in one of the sleepiest villages in England. Okay, so once in a while someone goes completely wild and parks on a yellow line but that's about it.

I mean, what did Joss expect? Shoot-outs at the Over-60's Club? Knife fights on the Bowling Green?

'Er, I'm not sure, Joss,' Miss Harris said, 'that we really need crime reporters for our little paper. You're not going to find much crime round here, are you?'

'But I already have!' shouted Joss. 'There's already been a crime. Last night! My next door neighbour, Mrs King, is dead . . . '

'Dead!' squealed Emma. 'You mean she was murdered?'

'Dead upset, I was going to say,' muttered Joss. 'About the robbery.'

'Robbery?' said Miss Harris. 'Poor Mrs King was robbed? Last night? That's terrible. What did they steal?'

'Er, something from the garden,' said Joss. 'They took Walter.'

'Who's Walter?' said Greg. 'A pet or something?'

'Well, no. He's not a pet exactly,' said Joss, more quietly. 'He's more of a . . .'

'What?' asked Greg, as everyone listened eagerly.

'A gnome,' Joss mumbled.

'A gnome!' I said. 'Someone's nicked a

garden gnome? Well, that's going to be front-page news, isn't it? We're going to have 'The News of the World' after that one, aren't we? I can see the headline now, *'Gnome-nappers terrorise village!'*

'Walter was Mrs King's favourite,' said Joss, as though that made all the difference.

'Great,' I said, 'perhaps the robber will send a ransom note, '£2,000 or the gnome dies!'

'It's a start,' Joss insisted. 'Gives us something to work on until we find something better.'

'We're not going to find anything better,' I groaned.

But Joss wasn't listening. He'd already started scribbling.

'Have you seen this one-legged gnome? 30cm tall. Wearing a red hat and green coat. Carrying a broken spade.'

'A broken spade?' I said. 'And only one leg?'

'Well it had two,' said Joss, 'until last month, when Mr King accidentally ran over it with his lawn mower.'

'Perhaps it wasn't an accident,' I said. 'Perhaps it was attempted murder. *Gnomicide!*'

'Shut up, Scott,' Joss moaned. 'You're not taking this seriously.'

Well no, I wasn't. But, unfortunately, Joss was. On the way home that Monday afternoon, he kept diving into bushes and peering over walls.

'It'll be a better story,' he informed me, 'if we can find Walter. Track down the thief.'

By this time Joss was actually rummaging through someone's dustbin so, I walked on, pretending I wasn't with him.

He'd gone completely crime crazy. Night after night, he carried on like that. He even bought a note-pad and made us both 'crime reporter' badges. I'd never seen him so keen on anything to do with school before.

Not that he was having much luck. There was no sign of Walter. But on Thursday Joss spotted something else, didn't he?

Chapter 2
The Break-in

It was 9 o'clock on Thursday night. We'd been at Greg's and we were walking home along Main Street. Joss was carrying his notebook and 'keeping his eyes peeled,' as he put it, when suddenly he stopped.

'Look at that,' he whispered.

'Look at what?' I said, half expecting to see someone rush past with a sack full of stolen gnomes.

'You're useless,' Joss said, pulling me into a doorway. 'You don't notice anything! Crime reporters have to stay alert. Now look over there.'

I looked. There was a blue car parked by the kerb. Next to it stood a man in a light jacket. He was looking at the big house on the corner.

'Yeah,' I said. 'So?'

'So that's the Clarke's place, isn't it?' Joss said. 'And they're in France, aren't they? So who's that man? And what's he doing there?'

'I don't know,' I said. 'Maybe he's a friend who doesn't know they're away.'

'So why's he acting so strangely?' said Joss.

I looked again and had to admit Joss had a point. The man was looking up and down the street. He walked towards the house. He stopped, turned and walked back to the car, still checking out the street.

Another man I'd never seen before, came out of the pub on the opposite corner. He looked around before hurrying over to the first man.

'See!' hissed Joss. 'That second bloke looks dead shifty.'

The man looked okay to me. Ginger-haired and wearing a nice suit. Quite ordinary, really.

'Narrow eyes,' said Joss peering at him. 'And thin lips. Sure signs of a criminal.'

'Don't be daft,' I said. 'You can't spot a criminal by the way they look.'

'Ssshh,' said Joss. 'They're going in.'

As soon as the man in the light jacket opened the gate, Joss pulled his phone from his pocket.

'What are you doing?' I asked.

'Phoning the cops.'

'Why?' I said. 'It's probably perfectly harmless.'

Only it didn't look at all harmless anymore. The men hadn't rung the doorbell or anything. While Joss was talking to the police, the men had disappeared round the back of the house.

'Come on,' said Joss.

'Er, where are we going?' I asked, as he started pulling me across the road.

'To keep an eye on things. Until the police turn up.'

No way did I want to go, of course. But there's no stopping Joss once he gets an idea in his head. He pushed me down beside the open gate. He gave me his note pad and told me to write down the car's number. Meanwhile, he crept up the path and peered through the window.

Minutes later, he was back. He squatted down beside me.

'They've broken in,' he whispered. 'There was a light on and I could hear them moving about. Where have the cops got to? They're going to be too late. Burglars don't hang around.'

Joss looked at the blue car. I got this sick feeling, even before he scuttled towards it, like a hunchback crab. He started unscrewing the tyre cap.

'Joss, you can't!' I said, following him.

'Why not?' he said. 'If we let the tyres down, they won't be able to get away, will they?'

'What if they come out?' I said, as my heart started to thud. 'What if they catch us? Couldn't we just get help from the pub or something?'

'They could have escaped by then,' Joss said. 'Come on, Scott. Do the back tyres.'

It's not easy letting air out of car tyres. And I don't suggest you try it. Especially after what happened to us.

We were listening to the air slowly hissing away, when we heard another noise. The sound of a door opening followed by a shout.

'Hey, you two! What do you think you're doing?'

Before we could think about moving, the burglars raced out of the Clarke's house. The ginger-haired one lurched at me, as I tried to scramble up. I rolled out of the way and he tripped over, landing on his bottom.

His legs were waving in the air and he was yelling some not very polite words.

'Run, Joss!' I called, getting to my feet.

But it was too late. The second man had already grabbed him.

Chapter 3
The Gnome Thief

What was I supposed to do? Tackle the burglar? Leave poor Joss and run for help?

As I stood there panicking, a police car swung round the corner. It skidded to a halt beside us. We were safe!

Two officers leapt out. A lady and podgy PC Drake, who comes into our school to give talks sometimes.

'I'll deal with this,' PC Drake said, pulling Joss away from the man.

'Let go,' Joss squealed. 'It's not me you want. It's them. The robbers!'

Only, by then, even Joss had noticed that the men weren't behaving much like criminals. The one who'd fallen over was on his knees, examining the flat tyres.

The other was shaking his head and looking very confused.

It was *so* embarrassing! PC Drake was very cross. He wasn't the least bit impressed by our 'crime reporter' badges.

When he took us home, our parents weren't exactly pleased with us either. Then there was more trouble the next day, when Miss Harris found out.

'Crime reporters,' she told us, 'are supposed to *report* crimes, not commit them!'

'Well, how were we supposed to know that the Clarkes had decided to rent out their house for the summer?' Joss moaned.

'And that the man in the light jacket was an estate agent! Fancy showing someone round at that time of night. It was bound to cause trouble.'

Not that my parents saw it that way. Especially when the estate agent phoned on Friday evening. He was yelling so loud, I could hear him from the other side of the room.

'Thanks to your son,' he shouted, 'the man I showed around decided not to rent the house after all. He said he didn't want to live in such a bad area full of thugs!'

Thugs?

Did he mean us?

My parents were in such a grump, they almost cancelled my sleepover with Joss on Saturday night. And looking back, of course, I wish they had.

I'd hoped all the trouble might have ended Joss's love of crime reporting. But no. On Saturday, he was round at Mrs King's pestering her for an update on the missing gnome. He spent most of the evening writing up his story.

'How about this?' he said. '*Villagers are living in fear, following a terrifying outbreak of gnome-napping and tyre slashing.*'

'Bit over the top,' I said.

'Yeah, well, all reporters do that, don't they?' he said, going back to his story. 'You have to make it sound exciting, don't you?'

Honestly, he was completely hooked. He had crime reporting on the brain. Which is why, when he woke me in the middle of the night, I didn't take much notice at first.

'Scott,' he hissed, 'wake up. There's something going on.'

'No there isn't!' I said. 'You've been dreaming.'

'Yes there is,' said Joss. 'There's someone in Mrs King's garden.'

I tried to ignore him but he dragged me out of bed. He pulled me over to the window.

I peered out and, to my amazement, Joss was right. There was someone creeping about in Mrs King's garden.

A tall figure, in a dark overcoat, carrying something under each arm. Two gnome-shaped objects!

'Great!' said Joss, 'he's come back for more gnomes. We've got him!'

'Hang on,' I said, 'what if we're making another mistake?'

'Don't be thick,' Joss snapped. 'It can't be a mistake this time, can it? We've caught him at it! You phone the cops and wake my parents. Do it quietly! And don't switch any lights on or he'll know we're onto him.'

Joss shoved his phone into my hand.

I still wasn't sure it was a good idea to phone the police but Joss had already gone. Seconds later, I heard the soft thud of his feet padding downstairs.

Surely he wasn't thinking of tackling a dangerous gnome thief? Not on his own! Joss hadn't left me any choice. I had to get help. So I made the call and stumbled out onto the landing to wake Joss's parents.

My bare foot touched something warm and furry. There was a loud yelp followed by my screams, as Joss's terrier leapt up at me.

'Down, Nipper,' I shouted.

So much for keeping quiet!

'What's going on?' said Joss's dad barging out of his bedroom.

He switched on the light.

Nipper started racing round in circles, barking.

'It's Joss,' I said, 'he's gone after the gnome thief.'

'He's done what?' said Joss's mum, appearing beside us.

There was no time to answer because of the clattering, shattering sound from outside, followed by the wail of a siren and a whole lot of shouting.

Nipper shot off downstairs. The front door was open and, by the time we got outside, there was a total riot going on in Mrs King's garden.

Chapter 4
A Surprise

Nipper had slipped through the fence, leapt into PC Drake's arms and was licking his plump face. Joss was picking up pieces of broken gnome from the path. People were peering out of their windows to see what was happening.

Mrs King rushed from her house shrieking at the top of her voice. She looked very silly in her nightdress, fluffy

slippers and pink hairnet but it was her
husband who was drawing everyone's
attention.

Mr King was wearing a long overcoat
draped over stripy pyjamas. He was sucking
his thumb, with his face glowing red in the
darkness. His whole body was puffing up,
like an excitable toad.

'He bit me!' he yelled, pulling his thumb out of his mouth. 'He bit my thumb!'

'Oh no!' said Joss's mum, 'that's not like Nipper. He never bites.'

'Not the dog,' boomed Mr King. 'Your son! He attacked me!'

'I'm sorry,' said Joss. 'But you scared me. I thought you were the gnome thief.'

'Gn . . . gnome thief!' spluttered Mr King.

'Well, what were you doing, Henry?' asked Mrs King. 'Creeping about in the middle of the night like that?'

'I had Walter mended,' said Henry King. 'And bought you another gnome. For your birthday. I wanted you to find them in the morning. It was meant to be a surprise.'

Surprise? Total shock was more like it. Poor Mr King had dropped both gnomes when Joss ran at him. We were in big trouble again, not least from Miss Harris on Monday morning.

'Do you realise,' she said, 'that both those gnomes are beyond repair.'

'We've offered to replace them,' I muttered.

'That,' Miss Harris snapped, 'is the least you can do! You will also be writing letters to say how sorry you are. You can write them instead of joining in with our newspaper project. And there will be no more crime reporting, do you understand?'

We nodded.

Joss looked as though he was going to cry when Miss Harris made us hand over our notebook and crime reporter badges.

I was more upset about having to replace the gnomes because they weren't cheap, were they? Oh, no. They were hand-painted.

£50 it was going to cost us. £50 each! Almost all the money I'd been saving up for a new skateboard.

On Wednesday, my mum took the afternoon off work. She was waiting outside school to drive us into town to get our money from the bank.

It was all right for Joss. He does a newspaper round and always has loads of money. But, as I stood at the cash-point, watching my notes come out, it was my turn to cry. £3.24 I had left. Great, I thought, as rain dripped down my neck, just great!

We splashed our way back to the car park, got in the car and set off down the high street.

'Only five o'clock,' Mum said. 'We could drive straight to the garden centre. Oh drat!'

'What?' I said.

'I forgot to pick up my watch from the jeweller,' she said. 'Hang on.'

She pulled into the kerb outside the jeweller's shop.

'Stay there,' she told us. 'I'll only be a minute. Look out for traffic wardens, I'm on a double yellow!'

'See, there's a crime,' I told Joss. 'Dangerous parking. Perhaps you could write about that.'

'No point,' said Joss, taking me seriously. 'We've been banned, remember? Besides, nearly everyone's handed their work in now. The deadline's tomorrow.'

He turned, staring miserably out of the back window.

'Hey,' he said. 'What the . . .'

There was no need to ask what he was shouting about. I'd already heard something speeding towards us. I turned, just in time to see a white van swerve in behind us and smack into our bumper.

There was a crunch and a jolt. My head snapped backwards then shot forward, as though it had ripped right off my neck. My nose banged against the seat, leaving me faint and dizzy. I heard the van's doors slam and felt Joss's nails digging into my arm.

'Scott,' he hissed, 'it's a raid. I think it's a raid. On the jeweller's.'

'Oh, give up, Joss,' I said, shaking him off.

I'd had enough! Some idiot had just damaged our car. My nose was bleeding and I felt too sick to listen to any more of Joss's stupid crime stories.

'Look!' he said, grabbing my sore head, forcing it upwards.

I looked, blinked and looked again. Four men from the van were heading towards the jewellers. Four masked men. All of them armed!

Chapter 5
Raiders

There was no mistake this time. A crime was taking place. A real crime. Right in front of our eyes. The air filled with screams, as shoppers froze for an instant, before diving for cover. A raider, with a shotgun, took up position outside the jeweller's.

A second raider smashed the window and started throwing trays of rings into a black bag.

But it was the other two who really
bothered me. The two with brown bags and
handguns, who burst into the shop, just as
an alarm started ringing.

'Mum!' I yelled, scrambling out of the car. 'My mum's in there!'

'Scott no!' I heard Joss shout.

It was a stupid thing to do. I can see that now. The most stupid thing I've ever done in my whole life. But, at the time, I didn't stop to think.

I raced forward but didn't get far. The man with the black bag swung round. The bag hit me in the stomach and I fell, banging my head on the pavement.

Above the sound of the alarm, I could hear sirens but all I could see was feet. Joss's trainers. Large, black boots running from the shop.

Joss tried to drag me back to the car.

'Grab the kids,' someone shouted.

The next thing I knew, I was pulled to my feet, by someone stronger than Joss, and thrown into the back of the van.

Joss was thrown on top of me, screaming and kicking. Two men leapt in. The door slammed and the van shot off with us rolling around, still screaming.

'Shut it,' a voice growled.

I felt Joss being pulled away from me. One of the men grabbed my hood and pulled me onto a low seat next to him.

On the seat opposite, sat Joss white and shivering. Next to him was a masked man, with a gun pointing at Joss's ribs. By their feet were two bags full of jewellery, glinting gold and silver.

There were no windows in the back of the van but I could tell it was travelling at terrific speed. It was bumping, jolting, swerving, making us slide up and down the seats.

'P . . . please,' I said to the man opposite. ' p. . .put the gun away. It might go off.'

'No it won't,' said the man next to me. 'None of the guns are real!'

'You're not supposed to tell them that,' his mate snapped.

'Oh, right, yeah, sorry! But I don't see why Ted made us bring the kids anyway.'

'Great!' said the other one. 'Tell the kids all our names, why don't you?'

'Sorry Uncle Rick!'

Rick growled. The one who kept giving away names rubbed his face and pulled off his mask.

'What do you think you're doing, you idiot?' said Rick.

'It's itching me!'

It was obvious why the mask was itching. His face was covered in spots. The sorts of spots teenagers get. He couldn't have been more than eighteen years old.

'Brilliant, Baz,' said Rick. 'So now the kids have seen you!'

'It doesn't matter,' growled a voice, as a panel slid open.

A man peered from the front of the van. He wasn't wearing his mask and I didn't much like what I saw.

This man was older. His face was hard; his eyes deep and mean.

'We've brought the boys as hostages,' he said. 'Cops won't bother us while we've got the kids. We can get rid of them later, when we burn the van.'

Get rid of us? Burn the van? Did he mean we'd be burnt with it? I couldn't help it. The sickness, lurking in the pit of my stomach, gushed up.

'Uggggh!' yelled Rick, as a fountain of vomit sprayed across onto his trousers.

He pulled off his mask, using it to wipe his trousers. Joss darted over and sat beside me. He clutched my arm, his fingers trembling.

'You two okay?' Baz asked, picking at the spot on his nose.

Stupid question, but he didn't seem as scary as the older men, so I nodded at him.

'My mum,' I managed to say. 'My mum was in the jeweller's. You didn't . . .'

'No,' he said. 'No one got hurt. You won't either if . . .'

'We'll see,' snarled the one in the front.

'You promised no one would get hurt, Ted,' Baz muttered.

'Yeah,' said Ted. 'But I didn't reckon on the cops arriving so quickly, did I? Or the kids getting in the way.'

'They're only about my brother's age,' said Baz. 'Promise you'll let them go.'

'All right,' sneered Ted. 'Scouts' honour. Will that do?'

'My mum said I shouldn't get mixed up with you lot,' Baz mumbled. 'She said it would lead to trouble. I wish . . . '

A burst of music silenced him. We all sat up, tense and alert. I stared, in horror, at my pocket. It was my phone. My phone was ringing.

'Answer it,' said Ted.

My hands were shaking so much I could barely hold on to it.

'Scott!' Mum screeched at me, almost shattering my ear drums. 'Where are you? They said you'd been kidnapped. It's not true. Tell me it's not true. Scott! Answer me!'

Chapter 6
Joss's Plan

Before I could say a word, Rick leant forward and grabbed the phone off me.

'He'll be fine, lady,' he said. 'As long as the cops keep away.'

Rick turned off the phone and put it in his pocket.

'Hand yours over,' he said to Joss.

Joss handed over his phone.

It seemed suddenly quiet inside the van. It took me a moment to work out why. The sounds outside had gone. The buzz of other traffic had gone, which probably meant we'd left town. More worrying was that the whirring overhead had gone as well.

'The police helicopter has pulled off,' the driver of the van shouted. 'Cars are still following but at a distance. Should be able to lose them now.'

The van shot forward even faster, if that was possible. Me and Joss clutched onto the seat as the van swung left, right, right, left, until we were completely dizzy.

I couldn't speak. Could barely think. Nothing seemed real. If anything, it was like watching a film. As though it was all happening to someone else. Not me.

'We've lost them,' I heard the driver shout.

'Okay,' said Ted. 'Time to change cars.'

He closed the panel and disappeared.

'Where are we going? Where are you taking us?' Joss asked.

'The less you know the better,' said Rick.

I stared at him, hoping that it was all, somehow, another mistake. Like the gnome thief and the estate agent. Maybe it really *was* a film and we'd got caught up in the action. But where were the cameras? Or maybe . . .

It was no good. I couldn't think of anything else. I had to accept that it was real. Horribly real.

A sharp jolt stopped me bursting into tears. It was followed by another and another as we all started to bounce up and down on the seats. We'd clearly left the road and were driving over rough ground.

Then we stopped. My heart almost stopped as well. I had to force myself to breathe as I heard the two men getting out of the front of the van. The back doors were flung open.

'Out,' Ted told us. 'Get out.'

We jumped down. Baz and Rick followed with the bags.

We were on a track. A muddy track. Lined with trees. Lots of trees. A wood then. We were in a wood. Miles away from anywhere. With no sound of sirens. No chance of rescue.

Ted pulled us away from the van.

There was a car parked in front. A red car, with someone in the driving seat, ready to whisk his friends away. But what about us? What were they going to do with us?

'Stand over there,' Ted said. 'Against that tree. Hands up. Don't move.'

He made us stand, facing the tree, with our hands above our heads. Behind me, I could hear the men rushing about. Throwing bags into the boot of the car. Bumping into each other. Swearing.

'This is a great story!' Joss whispered.

'What?' I said, barely able to believe my ears.

'Crime story,' Joss said, 'for our newspaper.'

Was he mad?

There we were, stuck in the middle of nowhere, with a gang of jewel thieves and

Joss thought it would make a nice story! He'd cracked up. The stress had completely squished his brain.

'If Miss Harris lets us,' said Joss. 'If we can make the deadline.'

'Deadline?' I hissed. 'Dead people, more like it. Because that's what we're going to be in a minute! Dead! And dead people don't write stories.'

'Ssshhh,' said Joss. 'Calm down. We're not going to die. I've got a plan.'

I hoped it wasn't like all his other crazy plans. Biting thumbs and letting tyres down.

'It better be good,' I said. 'Because this isn't Mr King you're dealing with. Or an estate agent. These men are dangerous.'

'I know,' whispered Joss, 'but they're also busy. Turn your head a bit and look.'

I turned. Joss was right. The men weren't watching us. They were changing their clothes. Throwing things into the back of the van. Pouring petrol over it!

'Whatever your plan is,' I said, 'you'd better make it quick.'

'No,' said Joss, quietly. 'Slow. We do everything slowly. Now keep your hands up and edge round the other side of the tree.'

We edged around. No one noticed.

Joss pointed to my feet then put his finger to his lips. Slow and quiet. That was the message. We were just going to slip away, as softly as melting snow.

And it might have worked.

Joss's plan might have worked.

Only Ted had quite a different plan in mind.

Chapter 7
On the Run

'Get the rope, Baz,' we heard Ted shout. 'I want those boys tied up.'

'Er, what boys?' someone said. 'They've gone!'

'Well get after them! Find them!'

That was it. No more creeping. We bolted off through the trees with the sound of footsteps thudding behind us.

On and on we ran, stumbling over
roots, pushing back branches that clawed at
our faces.

But where were we running to?

There was no sign of a path. Just
trees. Endless trees. Any minute now, the
men would catch up. Surround us. We could
hear them panting and shouting to each
other.

It was Joss's quick thinking that saved us. He dragged me into a tangle of bushes. He pulled me down with him, forcing me to lie flat and still. Not as easy as it sounds, as we were lying in a clump of nettles. They were sticking through my clothes. It felt like a million wasps stinging but I knew I didn't dare cry out.

'Er, they've disappeared,' said a voice, close by. 'Must be hiding.'

There was a snap, followed by rustling. A stick came poking into the bushes right next my head. My nose started to itch. I was going to sneeze. I screwed up my face, trying to stop myself. It was no good. Any minute now, the sneeze would burst out.

'Oh, leave them,' someone snapped.
'We haven't got time to mess about. By the
time they find their way out of the wood,
we'll have left the country, won't we?'

The stick was pulled away. Moving my
fingers really slowly, I pinched my nose
tight. The voices and footsteps started to
fade. We pulled ourselves up onto our knees
and peered out from the bush.

My nose had stopped itching, so I let
go.

'Aaaachoo!'

'What was that?' someone shouted. 'I
heard something! Back there.'

'It's all right, I'll go,' said another
voice.

We froze as we heard one set of footsteps crunching towards us. The footsteps stopped. The bushes parted. A face looked down at us. A spotty face.

Tears started to roll down my eyes. It was all over. We were going to die.

'What is it, Baz?' someone called.

Baz looked back towards the men, then down at us. He rubbed a spot on his chin, as if deciding what to do. The pause seemed to last forever.

'Nothing,' he shouted, 'it was a rabbit. Just a rabbit.'

Baz let the bush fall back into place. We heard him running to catch up with the others. Would he change his mind? Would he tell?

It seemed not. No one came back. Even so, we didn't dare move. Not straight away. Not until we were sure they'd gone.

'I think it's okay now,' Joss said.

We got up and scrambled out of the bushes. There was an enormous bang. We threw ourselves down again, clutching each other, shaking.

'The van,' said Joss. 'They've destroyed the van.'

When we finally got up again, we could see the smoke and the flames, even through the thick trees.

'What now?' I said. 'Head towards the flames? Back to the track? Try to find the way out?'

Even as I spoke, I knew I barely had the energy to move.

My skin was burning with nettle rash. I was dirty, wet and exhausted.

Baz had been kind. But he hadn't taken much of a risk, leaving us like that. It didn't matter that we knew their names. It didn't matter that we could describe them. By the time we found our way out, they would have escaped completely. If we ever found our way out!

'Joss,' I said. 'What if we're lost in here for days and days? What if . . .'

'Don't be daft,' said Joss. 'All we need to do is phone the cops. They'll be able to trace our signal, won't they?'

'Er, one slight problem,' I said. 'No phones! We gave them to the robbers, remember?'

'I gave them my old phone,' said Joss, taking out his new one from his pocket. 'Good job they didn't bother to search us, eh? Not very smart, were they?'

He leant against the tree, tapping the buttons on his mobile. He started talking to the police, giving a description of the men and their get-away car.

'That's right,' he was saying. 'Red Ford Focus. Registration number. . .'

I couldn't believe it. He'd actually checked the make of the car!

He knew the number!

'Joss,' I said, when he'd finished. 'That's amazing.'

'Not really,' said Joss, smugly. 'Crime reporters notice everything.'

Chapter 8
The Deadline

We headed towards the burning van.

'You lead the way,' Joss said. 'I'll phone our parents. Tell them we're okay.'

'Okay?' I said, feeling the scratches on my cheek with my swollen fingers. 'We've been kidnapped by jewel thieves and dumped in a wood. We're covered in cuts, stings and bruises. We were almost murdered! And you call that okay?'

'Could have been worse,' he said.

I opened my mouth, then closed it again. Joss was right. It could have been much worse.

About fifteen minutes later, our parents arrived with the police. There was a frenzy of hugs, squeals, tears and sloppy kisses. I thought my mum was going to squeeze me to death. She might have done if a policeman hadn't interrupted.

'We'll have to take a statement from you boys later,' he said. 'But first you should see a doctor. Get those injuries sorted out.'

'No time,' said Joss. 'We've got to write up our crime story. For the school newspaper. It's the deadline tomorrow.'

'No,' said his dad. 'No way! You're going
to the doctor and then you're going to get
some rest. You probably won't even be fit to
go to school tomorrow.'

'But Daaaad,' Joss wailed.

I don't know whether Joss got any rest but by 8 o'clock he was on the phone to me.

'Have you heard?' he screeched. 'They've got them. They've got the jewel thieves. The police caught up with them on the motorway. There was a chase and everything. I wish I'd been there. It sounded dead exciting. I've found out loads of stuff, for our story.'

I stood there, shaking my head. Would nothing put Joss off crime reporting?

'Both the van and the car were stolen,' he was saying. 'The police think it might be the same gang who robbed a jeweller's in Liverpool a couple of months ago. I want to get it all written up but Dad's making me go to bed!'

Personally, I couldn't wait to get to bed. But as soon as Joss hung up, the police arrived.

They asked me lots of questions. Stirring it all up again, so that by the time I finally got to bed, I couldn't sleep.

I lay there, going over it all. Most of all I thought about Baz. He'd been involved in a serious crime and that was wrong, of course. But I didn't think Baz was a really bad person and hoped the judge wouldn't be too hard on him when the case got to court.

Eventually I must have drifted off because the next thing I knew my mobile was ringing.

'Scott,' Joss yelled at me. 'Are you awake?'

'No,' I said. 'I always answer the phone in my sleep.'

'Do you know what time it is?'

I looked at my watch. Half past four.

'Joss, go away,' I groaned. 'It's the middle of the night.'

'No it isn't,' said Joss. 'It's half past four in the afternoon. Thursday afternoon. We've slept all day! And you know what that means, don't you?'

'Yes,' I said. 'It means we were very tired!'

'It means we've missed school,' said Joss. 'It means we haven't written our story. It means we've missed the deadline!'

I didn't much care about the story but Joss did.

Ten minutes later, he was round at my house.

'We'll write it anyway,' he said. 'Hand it in tomorrow. I'm sure Miss Harris will be able to squeeze it in. Right, I'll start with the raid. You can interview the kidnap victims.'

'But that was me,' I pointed out. 'How am I supposed to interview myself?'

'Easy,' said Joss. 'Just ask yourself questions and answer them. Now get a move on!'

On Friday morning, we were the first in school.

Joss raced up to Miss Harris.

'What do you think of this?' he asked, dropping two sheets of paper on her desk. 'Brave boys in kidnap drama.'

Miss Harris looked at our story.

'It's good,' she said. 'Very good. But I'm afraid . . . '

'Oh, Miss,' wailed Joss. 'We're not still banned are we? This is a real crime story.'

'No, you're not banned,' said Miss Harris. 'You're just too late. Our newspaper's being printed right at this moment.'

Joss's face started to crumple.

'I'm sorry,' Miss Harris said. 'I'm so sorry. But there's nothing I can do. We can't make any changes now.'

'I don't believe it!' said Joss. 'We went through all that and didn't even get our story in the paper. We missed the deadline!'

Chapter 9
The Summer Gala

Joss was in no hurry to get to the gala on Saturday, so we went to the garden centre first.

We bought two gnomes for Mr and Mrs King. I tried not to be too upset as I handed over all my money. After all, it was our fault that the gnomes got broken. So it was only fair that we paid for them.

The Kings were ever so pleased when we took the gnomes round. Mr King seemed to have forgotten all about his sore thumb.

'You're good lads. Remembering our gnomes after the excitement you've had. I read all about it in the local paper,' he said.

'What?' said Joss.

'The Herald,' said Mr King, picking up a copy from the table. *High Street Jewel Raid - Robbers caught.'*

'It's not fair,' said Joss. 'That's my story. They've stolen my story! I missed the school deadline and now it's in The Herald. It's not fair!'

He was even more upset when we read the story. It hardly mentioned us at all! Just the fact that we'd had a lucky escape.

By the time we got to the gala, Joss was in a real grump especially when Emma tried to sell him a copy of the school newspaper. He wasn't interested in any of the stalls.

'Oh come on,' I said. 'Let's try Penalty Shoot Out. That should cheer you up.'

We were about to move when someone came up behind us, clamping heavy hands on our shoulders.

'So,' said PC Drake, waddling in front of us. 'You found your crime story after all.'

'Fat lot of good it did us,' said Joss.
'We missed the deadline.'

'Oh,' said PC Drake. 'Never mind. At
least there's the reward to look forward to.'

'Reward?' I said.

'Didn't you know?' said PC Drake. 'The jeweller's giving you a reward of £200.'

'£200!' I shrieked.

'Each,' he said.

'Each!' I said.

'Do you have to repeat everything?' Joss muttered. 'You sound like a mad parrot.'

Can you believe it? Even the thought of a £200 reward hadn't cheered Joss up. Neither did the Penalty Shoot Out. Joss could barely be bothered. He sent one ball so wide that it knocked two coconuts off the coconut shy.

His second shot landed on the school roof and his third almost killed a sparrow.

All three of mine went in but I didn't have time to collect my prize because Joss pulled me away. He pointed at a man dressed in black, with a bag over his shoulder.

'It's him,' said Joss.

'Who?' I said.

'The thief,' Joss muttered.

Thief? What thief? The raiders had all been arrested, so what on earth was Joss on about now?

'I don't care who he is,' I said. 'I

don't care if he's Jack the Ripper. Just leave him alone. We've finished with crime reporting. It's over. Joss, are you listening?'

Joss wasn't. He rushed up to the man.

'It's you!' Joss said. 'Isn't it?'

'Probably,' said the man, smiling. 'Ben Perkins. Reporter. Weekly Herald.'

'Told you,' said Joss, turning to me. 'Told you he was a thief, didn't I? He's the one who stole our crime story.'

'Your crime story?' said Ben.

Joss scowled at him, so I explained about the school newspaper and missing the deadline.

'I know what you mean,' Ben said. 'Deadlines are a problem. I only just got my story in on time. So I was hoping to do a follow-up next week. About you boys. How your quick thinking led to the capture of the raiders. If I could ask you a few questions . . . '

'No,' said Joss, sulkily. 'Don't see why we should tell you anything. It was our story.'

'Pity,' said Ben, 'because I was going to invite you into The Herald, for a day, to have a look round and maybe help me. But if you're not interested . . . '

He started to walk away.

'Wait,' shouted Joss. 'You mean I can be a real crime reporter? On a real paper? For a whole day? Yesssss!'

We went to The Herald on Wednesday.

I thought Joss was going to die of excitement, especially when Ben let us write up some of the story on his computer.

On Friday, we got our £200 reward and I bought my skateboard.

As for Joss, well there was only one thing in the whole world he really wanted . . .

. . . a copy of The Herald with his story on the front page!

PUBLISHING